MULLAH NASRUDIN IS ALIVE AND WELL

Cross-Cultural Communications
Merrick, New York
2022

Gabriel Rosenstock

Cross-Cultural Communications
Stanley H. Barkan, Editor-Publisher
239 Wynsum Avenue Merrick, NY 11566-4725/USA
Tel: 516/868-5635 Fax: 516/379-1901
Email: cccpoetry@aol.com

ISBN 978-0-89304-620-0

Library of Congress Control Number: 2022930276

CONTENTS

In Memoriam
Idries Shah
(Simla, British India, 1924 - London, 1996)

BANANA

Nasrudin found a banana. It must have fallen off the back of a truck. Dutifully, he brought it home to his wife.

'Some husbands bring home flowers,' she sighed. 'You bring a banana.'

'Do flowers have Vitamin B6, beloved? Also, did you know that you can polish your teeth with a banana skin?'

'Now it's my teeth, is it? Anything else?' she asked dryly.

'If you discard the skin carelessly, my dear, one of us might slip – which would be a great source of mirth to the other – and Allah knows we need a good laugh in these strange times.'

THE JOYS OF READING

'Wife!' said the Mullah, 'it's time you learned how to read.'

'It is?' Fatima was utterly astounded.

'It is!' exclaimed the Mullah. 'I'm thinking of writing a book – and I'm sure it would do you a lot of good to read it!'

'That's all fine and dandy, Nasrudin,' she replied. 'But first *you're* going to have to learn how to write!'

POOP

A group of children were following Nasrudin as he walked down the street with his head held high. The children were laughing loudly. A bird had pooped on Nasrudin's turban. The kids followed him all the way to the dry cleaners.

'And how do you intend to pay for this, Nasrudin?' asked the cleaner.

'Barter!' came the instant reply.

'Barter?' asked the cleaner.

'Listen to them! Is not the laughter of children the most precious thing in the world?'

A FISHERMAN'S TALE

The Chief of Police and the Mullah went fishing one day. After an hour, the Chief caught a rainbow trout.

'Well done!' said the Mullah Nasrudin, flattering him.

The Chief examined it, forensically.

'I don't like the look of it, Mullah. Or the smell. Something fishy about it.'

'Well, it is a fish after all,' said the Mullah, philosophically.

'Does the tail look rotten to you?' The policeman sniffed.

'The tail? How could it be rotten? It's fresh out of the river. And anyway, a fish is like a country . . .'

'In what way, Mullah?'

'It always rots from the head down.'

THE MULLAH DINES OUT

Mullah Nasrudin decided he would give himself a treat. Having saved up for about a year and a half, he now had enough money in his monkey-bank. (He abhorred 'piggy banks' and anything related to pork.) This evening he would dine out, alone, and savour his own thoughts.

The waiter arrived with the wine list.

'No wine, thank you! I'm driving.'

The waiter – and the rest of the staff – knew very well that he had arrived by donkey, a donkey by the name of Winston. He then presented the menu to his ravenous guest, with an extravagant flourish:

'May I recommend the pork belly with fennel seeds, thyme and . . .'

'You may not!' thundered the Mullah who had his belly full of people suggesting this and that and the other. Was he not perfectly capable of making up his own mind on culinary matters, matters political, scientific and metaphysical? He was a Mullah, after all. Not an unlettered peasant.

'I'll have the unlettered pheasant, please.'

'Excellent choice. And how would you like it?'

'Immediately.'

No hanging around for the Mullah. As he found that he had no thoughts to savour, he decided he would skip dessert and coffee.

When he finished off the pheasant, he beckoned to the waiter, indicating that he wished to pay.

The Mullah promptly paid his bill and fumbled in his pocket for some small change. Then he rose to leave.

The waiter looked coldly at the measly tip and muttered under his breath:

'Tip of the iceberg.'

LOVE

The Mullah ordered another coffee and when Ahmed, manager and proprietor of the Fancy Sandwich Bar (FSB), brought it to him, the Mullah gestured to him to come close, indicating that he had some very important secret to impart. Whereupon, the Mullah, clutching Ahmed feverishly, kissed him boldly on the lips. Twice.

Ahmed coughed and spluttered.

'Mullah! What the –?'

'Hmm . . .' said the Mullah. 'It's not true then . . .'

'What's not true?'

'Something I heard this morning on the radio. *All the world loves a lover.*'

Then he quickly changed the subject. 'What does FSB stand for, Ahmed? I've forgotten.'

'Forgotten Sandwich Bar. Everything that happens here is forgotten, Nasrudin.'

ON BEING SOMEONE ELSE

'Well,' says the Chief Justice, if it's not my old friend, Mullah Nasrudin!'

'And if it's *not*?' asked Nasrudin, gloomily.

'Then it must be someone else.'

'How I wish I *were* someone else!' said Nasrudin, not without a touch of self-pity.

'Really?'

'I was at the barber this morning.'

'Really?'

'Well, not that it's obvious, what with the turban and all that. Anyway, there was a song on the radio, Your Honour. The singer was a certain Paul McCartney. Have you heard the name? Quite famous, I believe.'

'Oh, really?'

'Anyway, this McCartney fellow was singing the praises of some Mullah or other and I said to myself, why doesn't anyone sing about me? I mean, who has ever heard of that other Mullah? You should have heard the praise heaped upon him!'

'Really?'

'Unbelievable, Your Honour:

> *Nights when we sang like a heavenly choir*
> *Of the life and the times of the Mullah Kintyre'.*

TO THE BEACH

Nasrudin was doing some repairs when he discovered a little pouch. It contained a substantial amount of money.

'I don't believe it! Must have belonged to a previous owner,' he mused.

'Wife, we're off to the beach for the day!'

'The beach? Oh, Nasrudin! I haven't been to the beach for donkey's years.'

'Shhh . . . don't say that! Winston might hear you!'

Twenty minutes later, the taxi arrived.

'To the beach!' instructed Nasrudin, speaking and behaving like a playboy or celebrity who has nothing to do but go to the beach every day.

And off they went, Nasrudin whistling gaily to himself. Fatima said she was looking forward very much to having an ice-cream. She hadn't tasted one in yonks.

'Any flavor you like, *ma chérie.*'

'Cherry? Oh yes, that would be nice.'

They were so taken up in their anticipation of their day out together that they hardly noticed the landscape whizzing by, or the sudden change in the weather.

It began to rain. A light drizzle at first. Soon it turned into a downpour.

'By the way, Nasrudin, how can we afford this? Isn't it rather extravagant?'

Nasrudin told her about his little stroke of luck.

'A pouch? A little green pouch? Nasrudin! That was my escape money! Taxi! Stop! Turn back.'

'Escape money?' exclaimed Nasrudin. 'What do you mean? Escape from what?'

'From you! Taxi, stop! Turn back.'

'But we're here,' said the driver, stopping.

'Here? What do you mean?' said Nasrudin, peering through the fogged up windscreen.

The driver pointed to a lone tree in a field.

'There!' he said. 'Look! The beech!'

MOUSETRAP

'What is all that noise?'

'Don't worry, wife. I'm building something.'

'You are a builder now? What is it you're building?'

'What does it look like?'

'No idea.'

'A mousetrap.'

Fatima was flabbergasted.

'Say that again?'

'Shh . . . the walls have ears.'

'Mullah . . . *why* are you building a mousetrap?'

'For you, beloved.'

'For   me?   I   need   a   mousetrap?'

'You think I'm doing this for myself? For my own amusement? I'm doing this for us!'

'Us?'

'Yes beloved . . . something I heard on the radio. I paid no attention to it at first. Then the penny dropped.'

'I see. And what did you hear on the radio?'

'*Build a better mousetrap and the world will beat a path to your door.*'

WINSTON IN TROUBLE AGAIN

'Your Honour! Before you pronounce sentence . . .'

'Speak!' said the Chief Justice.

'You Honour, I would ask you to repeat the charges made against my donkey in the animal's presence.'

'This is a very unusual request, Mullah Nasrudin . . .' He thought for a while.

'Your request is granted. Let Winston be brought before the bench.'

Winston was ushered in, bribed by a carrot.

'Is Winston ready to hear the charges brought against him, Mullah? asked the Chief Justice, solemnly.

'He is all ears, Your Honour.'

BAD ODOUR

Nasrudin went for a sandwich. He spotted the Chief Justice at the other end of FSB but decided not to greet him as he looked decidedly down in the dumps. Stomach trouble again, no doubt. Poor CJ was, in his own words, 'A martyr to gas.'

After a while, an unpleasant odour assailed Nasrudin's nostrils. What was it? Sewage? Something that had gone off?

Ahmed noticed it as well.

'What the hell is it, Mullah? Any idea?' he asked Nasrudin.

'I think it's coming from the Chief Justice,' whispered Nasrudin.

'Why would you say that?' whispered Ahmed.

'Look around. He's the only big cheese in here.'

'This place will quickly become known as the Farting Sandwich Bar,' said Ahmed.

POLICE RAID

The Chief of Police arrived with a motley crew of junior policemen and one policewoman. The neighbours gathered, as was their wont any time Nasrudin's house was raided.

'I'm coming!' shouted Nasrudin, 'you don't have to knock the door down.'

Nasrudin opened the door, gingerly.

'Oh, it's you,' he muttered, darkly.

'Yes,' said the Chief, 'who were you expecting? The Shah of Persia?'

'Are you alone in the house?'

'Yes. My wife has gone to stay with her mother. You just missed her!'

'Her mother is still alive?'

'As far as I know.'

'May we come in?'

'What? All of you? Not without a warrant. What do you want?'

'We've had complaints,' said the Chief, icily.

'I'm not surprised,' remarked Nasrudin, sarcastically. 'Everyone is complaining. We need a change of government. That's what we need. So, what was the nature of the complaint this time, may I enquire?'

'Booze.'

'Booze? You are mistaken. No booze in this house. This is a respectable house. My wife and I are God-fearing people. I have character references galore. The Chief Justice himself has attested to –'

'Yeah, yeah, your fishing buddy, we know.'

'I have gone fishing with you as well, don't forget.'

'Don't muddy the waters, Nasrudin. Your favourite trick! Here is a transcript of the complaint. I have underlined the relevant section: lots of booze! Now, what do you have to say to that, eh?'

'It's obviousthatyou– oroneofyourincompetentunderlings – misheard the complaint and it was faultily transcribed, I regret to say.'

'Misheard the complaint? Are you serious, Nasrudin?'

The eyes of the Chief of Police narrowed suspiciously.

'Of course I'm serious! Have you ever known me not to be?' The police looked at each other knowingly.

'I was in the bath,' explained Nasrudin.

The policewoman was seen to blush.

'Don't muddy the waters, Nasrudin!' warned the Chief.

'I began to sing. Like a bird. I do a rather decent rendering of Nessun Dorma, if I say so myself.'

The Chief threw his eyes to heaven. Nasrudin burst into song, addressing the policewoman as though she were the princess mentioned in Puccini's aria:

> Nessun dorma, nessun dorma
> Tu pure, o, Principessa
> Nella tua fredda stanza
>> Guardi le stelle che tremano
>> D'amore e di speranza . . .

'Enough!' cried the Chief. The policewoman was about to applaud but thought better of it.

Nasrudin acknowledged her unspoken admiration, much to the annoyance of the others.

'Not everyone is as appreciative as you, Principessa! Take my wife, for instance. She boos me every time I sing.' He turned to the Chief. 'Might that give you a little hint? Boos? Oh yes, lots and lots of boos . . .'

BLESSINGS

The Mullah's nearest neighbour, Siraj, called to the door, looking for the loan of a screwdriver. The Mullah didn't even look at him, his gaze to heaven, slowly counting out loud:

'93 . . . 94 . . .'

'Mullah, are you all right?'

'98 . . . 99 . . .'

'Mullah?'

Siraj ran off and before long the whole neighbourhood had gathered. There was the Mullah, at the front door, counting sheepishly.

'He's lost it this time. Completely bonkers.'

'It was inevitable, wasn't it?'

'Runs in the family. Bad genes.'

'A mullah should not wear jeans in the first place!'

'125 . . . 126 . . . . . . 127.'

Children giggled, others whispered among themselves.

The schoolteacher arrived. People asked him did he think the Mullah was having a mental breakdown.

'It could very well be,' said the schoolteacher. 'However, I have heard of Sufi poets who were unable to express themselves in words. They had, so to speak, gone beyond words. They could only come out with various numbers, finally ending up with the number 1.'

'148 . . .'

The Mullah stopped suddenly. There was a hush.

Would he start again?

The schoolteacher tentatively approached the Mullah.

'Everything OK, Mullah?'

'Yes, teacher, fine. Why do you ask?'

'We were worried. All those numbers.'

'Ah, yes,' said the Mullah. 'It was something I heard on the radio.'

'On the radio?'

'Yes.'

'What did it say?'

'Count your blessings.'

ANOTHER DAY IN THE FANCY SANDWICH BAR

There had been a lot of talk recently about constitutional change. Some judges were for it, others against it. Ahmed cupped his hand before his mouth and asked Nasrudin what he thought the Chief Justice's attitude to the proposed changes might be.

CJ was in the corner, quietly sipping his coffee, engrossed in an editorial in *The Times*.

'Look at him, Ahmed!' said Nasrudin, with a sort of friendly contempt. 'I wouldn't expect much from that fellow – day in, day out, always behind the times.'

BUSY

The Chief of Police decided to call on the Mullah, personally, to investigate complaints about loud noise – hammering – and what appeared to be an abnormal amount of mice running around the place.

The Mullah was on his knees, on a small patch of grass in front of his house, with a scissors.

What was he up to? The Chief forgot what brought him there in the first place. His eyes nearly popped out of his head when it became clear that the Mullah was cutting the grass with a little nail scissors.

'Everything OK, Mullah?'

'Of course!'

'What exactly are you doing, Mullah?'

The Mullah looked up from his work:

'Have you never heard the expression – don't let the grass grow under your feet?'

DAILY CHALLENGES FACING THE MULLAH

His monkey-bank was empty. Nothing. Not even a peanut. He went to the fridge.

'Wife!' shouted the Mullah. 'The fridge is empty again!'

'My life is empty!' sighed the Mullah's wife.

'What on earth do you mean?'

'Mullah! You were supposed to learn how to write. Yes? Then you were going to write a book. Yes? Everyone was going to read it! Yes? You promised we would have new clothes. Yes? Plenty food in the fridge. Yes?'

'Yes! Well . . . that's a lot of yesses, isn't it, beloved? When did I ever say, No?'

She began to cry.

'Wife, you must understand, I am a devout Muslim. It's not easy for me to bring home the bacon.'

BE CAREFUL!

'There you are, Nasrudin!' exclaimed the Chief Justice.

'Your Honour!'

'How is Winston?'

'Fine, fine.'

'And your wife? Fatima, is it?'

Nasrudin thought for a minute.

'Yes, yes, Fatima Fatima, she is fine too.'

'Good good! Nasrudin, you are a man about town . . .'

'In a manner of speaking.'

'What are people saying about the forthcoming election? I have some friends in high places who are very anxious to know what the general feeling is among the citizenry. There isn't any swing . . .' and he moved his left hand cautiously across the table.

'Swing? To the right?'

'That's your right. My left, Nasrudin!'

'Left? Oh, yes of course. I mean, no – they've all moved so far to the right, they don't even know where left is anymore!'

'Good, good.'

'They don't really care who wins: the general feeling is that the government always gets in.'

'Hmm . . . on another matter: I would like you to warn your fellow citizens that there's a cat burglar in the district.'

'How awful!' exclaimed the Mullah.

'Yes, and a particularly clever cat burglar at that. So be careful! And please warn others.'

'I certainly will. Lucky me, not having a cat, Your Honour!'

HELP

When Fatima informed him that the fridge was empty (again), Nasrudin rode to market.

He saw mountains of juicy cherries and was quite dazzled by the sight.

'I'll have some cherries, please.'

'Help yourself,' said the stallholder and continued with her knitting.

Nasrudin filled a bag and walked away, whistling.

'Stop thief!' cried the stallholder and before long a security guard had Nasrudin by the scruff of the neck.

'How dare you?' exclaimed Nasrudin.

'How dare *I*, is it? You think you can just come here and help yourself to whatever you want?'

'Of course!' replied Nasrudin, vehemently, 'God helps those who help themselves.'

A DONKEY RIDE TO NOWHERE

The Chief Justice rang the Mullah:

'Get your ass over here.'

'Do you mean my posterior, i.e. my good self or Winston?'

'All three! My donkey, Rumi, is washed and combed already. We're going for a ride.'

CJ and the Mullah often went off together, into the wilderness.

'You know, Mullah, they have a car at my disposal all the time but there is nothing – I repeat nothing – to compare with a donkey ride in the country. I find it extremely therapeutic!'

'I wonder how your Rumi finds it,' thought Nasrudin to himself. (CJ was 18 stone, at least, and prone to sudden gas emissions).

They came to a river. It was flooded.

'What do we do now?' moaned CJ. 'I don't want to go back!' He was like a child. Donkey rides brought out the child in him.

'Don't worry, Your Honour! We'll cross that bridge when we come to it . . .'

'But – dash it all, Nasrudin – we have come to it!'

ART FOR ART'S SAKE

'There's money in art, wife,' said the Mullah, thoughtfully. 'I saw in the paper that a man called Scully sold a painting for 2 million –that's dollars, not dinars. How many fridges could you fill with that? How many burkas could you buy?'

'I have enough burkas, thank you. By the way, I didn't know you could read, Mullah,' said his wife, the long-suffering Fatima.

'It was read out to me, wife.'

'Anyway, it's all fake news, Mullah.'

'Be that as it may. I'm taking up art.'

A month later, Fatima asked.

'How's the art going? May I see what you have drawn?'

She had a peep. The canvas was untouched.

'What's this, Mullah?'

'Hmm . . .' he replied, 'I seem to be drawing a blank.'

HASTE

Nasrudin's donkey, Winston, fouled the street again. This time the Chief of Police himself was witness to the crime. He measured the offending item.

'Fifteen inches, Nasrudin. Fifteen inches of filth!' He glared at Nasrudin, then glared at the donkey. The donkey glared back. Neither of them blinked.

'I'm sorry,' said a sheep-faced Nasrudin. 'We were in a bit of a hurry.'

'In a bit of a hurry? What has that got to do with it?'

'Have you never heard the expression, *Haste makes waste*?'

IS THE AYATOLLAH A CATHOLIC?

After a glorious day donkey-riding in the hills, the Chief Justice invited the Mullah back to his place for some refreshments.

'Whiskey?' asked the host.

'Alcohol, Your Honour?! But isn't it forbidden?'

'Mullah! I am a judge, am I not? How am I to know about the evils of alcohol? From a book?'

'So, we're going to get drunk?'

'You betcha! Ossified!'

The Mullah savoured the whiskey.

'Scotch, Your Honour?'

'Irish.'

'The Irish make whiskey?'

'Is the Ayatollah a Catholic?'

'What? The Ayatollah is a Catholic?'

'Of course! But . . . let that be our little secret, Mullah.' The Chief Justice gestured to his host to zip his lips.

'My lips are sealed, Your Honour.'

After a while, the host noticed that his guest wasn't drinking.

'Not to your taste, Mullah?'

The Mullah replied, hardly opening his mouth at all.

'My lips are sealed, Your Honour. . .'

STRICT DIET

The Chief Justice visited the Mullah in prison.

'Your trial is tomorrow, my friend. I'm bound by law to issue the death penalty, but after careful consideration, I have decided to let you off with a warning.'

'You are very kind.'

'Not at all, Mullah. What are friends for?'

The following day, the Mullah was accused of fouling the street – for a second time.

'Not me!' protested the Mullah. 'It was my donkey!'

'Sure! That was your excuse the first time, Mullah. This time, however, we sent the specimen for analysis. The lab reported finding dates, humus, olives and pomegranate seeds in the offending specimen. You feed such delicacies to your donkey?'

The Mullah hung his head in shame.

'What was I to do?' he lamented. 'I was caught out!'

'Yes, *I* caught you!' exclaimed the Chief of Police, grinning from ear to ear.

'Any more outbursts and I will clear the court!' thundered the Chief Justice.

Under his greasy moustache, the Chief (of Police) curled his lip contemptuously.

'Hardly an outburst,' he muttered.

'Let me be the judge of that!'

Turning to the accused, CJ intoned, gravely:

'The law recommends 90 lashes for the first fouling and the death penalty for a second offence.'

'I daren't think what the punishment might be for a third offence,' said the Mullah, casually.

'Silence – or you will be in contempt of court!'

Following a pregnant silence, CJ spoke:

'It is a matter of public knowledge that this city does not have enough public conveniences. I have decided, therefore, to be lenient, Mullah. I am letting you off with a warning. You have been warned, Mullah. Do you understand?'

'You betcha, Your Honour. Pomegranate seeds? Hah! From now on it's strictly carrots for me!'

JOKE

'Hail fellow well met!' said the Chief Justice, as Nasrudin joined him in the Fancy Sandwich Bar.

'May I order you a coffee, Mullah?'

'You may, Your Honour. I'm in need of a bit of a boost.'

'Oh, why is that?'

'I don't know. I am prone to . . . my shrink calls it ontological insecurity.'

The Chief Justice ordered two coffees.

'You can afford a shrink?'

'He does it for nothing, Your Worship. He says I'm a unique case. He's writing a book about it.'

'I see . . . I don't know why you should feel insecurity, of all things. You are quite famous. Did you know that?'

'Famous?' The Mullah was astounded.

'Oh yes, people tell funny stories about you.'

'They do?'

'Sure, all the time. You want to hear one?'

'Er . . . I'm not sure if I do . . . Well, go on, yes. Let's hear one, then.'

'OK . . . here we go. One day, the Mullah Nasrudin brought his donkey, Winston, to the blacksmith.'

'They mention my name? They say Mullah Nasrudin?'

'Yes.'

'Does my wife know about this?'

'I don't know. Yes, more than likely. Now be quiet and listen to the joke. He brings Winston to the forge . . .'

'*I* bring Winston to the forge, you mean.'

'No more interruptions! Please! And the blacksmith says, Mullah, what can I do for you?'

'I would like my donkey to be shoed,' said the Mullah.

'Sure,' said the blacksmith. The whites of his eyes were emphasized by his sooty face; he began to wield his tongs fiercely at the poor donkey.

'Shoo! Shoo!' shouted the blacksmith and the Mullah's donkey ran away, braying his head off.

'Ha ha!'

Nasudin laughed:

'Ha ha ha!'

CJ laughed again:

'Ha ha ha ha!'

Nasrudin continued laughing:

'Ha ha ha ha ha ha!'

Everyone in FSB began to stare at them.

The Chief Justice stopped laughing and composed himself.

'OK, that's enough, Nasrudin. Nasrudin! Stop! Stop laughing!'

'Ha ha ha ha ha ha!' laughed Nasrudin.

'Stop it!'

'Ha ha ha ha ha ha ha! ha! He who laughs last laughs loudest!'

SPOON

The Mullah went to the blacksmith.

'Good morning, smithy!'

'Mullah! What brings you here?'

'Ah, my good friend, they are telling lies about us.'

'Oh, you mean the joke about . . . It's only a joke, Mullah. You are not offended, surely?'

'Personally, I am not offended. But I don't know what Winston thinks about the matter.'

'Of course . . .'

'Smithy, could you make me a long spoon?'

'A long spoon, Mullah? What an unusual request.

Of course I can make you a long spoon. How long?'

'Long,' answered the Mullah. 'May I collect it this time tomorrow morning? And I don't expect you to charge me . . . after the humiliation suffered by Winston.'

The blacksmith thought better of arguing with the Mullah and had the spoon ready for him the following morning.

One o'clock in the afternoon and Nasrudin heads for the FSB. Saturday. The Chief Justice could always be found there at lunchtime on Saturdays, enjoying a bowl of soup.

Nasrudin joined him and the two of them were presented with two large bowls of steaming chicken noodle soup.

'Yummy!' said the Chief Justice. His troublesome belly rumbled.

Nasrudin produced the long spoon.

'My goodness!' exclaimed the Chief Justice. ' Look at the length of that spoon!'

'Have you never heard the expression, He who sups with the devil should have a long spoon?'

THE SHRINK

'Nice to see you again,' said the shrink.

'Nice to be back,' said Nasrudin as he lay back on the couch.

'Ah,' he sighed, 'I love this couch. I don't know what you are doing to my head, doctor, but this couch works wonders for my back.'

'Shall we start?' asks the shrink.

'I think I shall conduct this session myself.'

'What do you mean?'

'I mean, *I'll* ask the questions: now Nasrudin, when did you first notice that Winston was listening in to conversations you were having with your wife?'

'Hold on a minute,' said the shrink. 'I don't think this is going to work . . .'

'Why not? Have you never heard it said, *If you want a thing done well, do it yourself.*'

JAM

'I'll tell you what I'll do, beloved' said Nasrudin to his wife, 'I'll pop down now to the FSB and have myself a slice of toast. Then I'll ask Ahmed for some jam – and then I'll being home the jam! You see? You can eat it with the long spoon, if you like. What do you fancy? Apricot? Would you like some apricot jam?'

'Anything at all,' said Fatima, the embodiment of living martyrdom.

Nasrudin's toast arrived.

'Would you have some jam to go with that, Ahmed?' he asked nonchalantly.

Ahmed shook his head.

Nasrudin's eyes widened.

'What? No jam? And you call yourself the Friendly Sandwich Bar?'

'You know the saying, Mullah:
Jam tomorrow, and jam yesterday, but never jam today.'

HAPPINESS

'Are you happy?' asked the shrink.
'Am I happy? Happy as a clam,' said Nasrudin.
'Happy as a clam? What does that mean?'
'I don't know,' answered Nasrudin.
'You don't know?'
'No.'
'Are you clamming up on me?'

ENGLAND

Oh to lie awake at night and think of England,
Out of reach and far away;
Oh, to see her in the distance as a picture,
And let your fancy play.

Nasrudin whispered sweet nothings into Fatima's shell-like ear but she seemed to be very far away.

'Darling? Fat? Earth to wife! Come in wife . . . You seem so distant!'

'I was thinking of England.'

'England? Huh! Well, lie back and think of England then – what do I care!'

FATHER

'Tell me a little bit about your father,' asked the shrink.

'There's not much to tell,' said Nasrudin. 'He didn't know whether to scratch his watch or wind his ass.'

'I see. And your mother?'

'She scratched his watch for him.'

WIND

Nasrudin arrived at the FSB and Ahmed took him aside.

'I wouldn't sit with your friend CJ this morning, if I were you,' he advised. 'Definitely not.'

'Oh?' asked Nasrudin.

'He's been farting loudly for the past 10 minutes and by all appearances, it looks like he's getting a second wind.'

'Well, I'm certainly not going to steal his thunder!' said Nasrudin.

TIME

A crowd had gathered around Nasrudin. One could always depend on Nasrudin to put on a good show.

They watched him closely as he walked up and down, firmly clutching an alarm clock. What was he up to?

He stopped and suddenly hurled the clock with great force against a wall. A cheer arose from the crowd.

It wasn't long before the police arrived; the Chief of Police himself made an appearance. He had a keen interest in Nasrudin's antics. (In fact, it is said he was keeping a diary which he intended to publish some day.)

Nasrudin picked up the battered clock, walked back ten paces, and promptly hurled the clock against the wall again.

Once more he tramped back to the wall and was about to pick up the battered clock again when the Chief of Police stopped him.

'Nasrudin!' he said, 'what do you think you are doing?'

'Nothing,' said Nasrudin, 'just killing time.'

HONEY

'There's nothing in the house! Not a crumb of bread, Nasrudin! Nothing. Have you no shame! Go! This minute! Go and bring back something, or I won't be here when you get back.'

'Well, if you're not going to be here when I get back, what's the –'

'Go!'

Nasrudin rushed out the door with his tail between his legs. Soon he and Winston were raising dust on the road.

On the way, they met a honey-seller who had 10 jars of honey he was hoping to sell at the market.

'I'll get you to the market in double-quick time for just one of those jars of honey,' said Nasrudin. 'Hop up behind me.'

The honey seller agreed and wasn't put off by Winston's unwelcoming stare. Once they reached the market and deposited their passenger, Nasrudin headed for home with the honey.

'Honey you have brought back?' said Fatima, incredulously. 'Honey?!'

'Well, you know what they say, darling . . .'

'What do they say?'

'You can catch more flies with honey than you can with vinegar!'

MARRIAGE

'Sorry for keeping you waiting, Mullah,' said the shrink. 'I was with my shrink.'

'You see a shrink?'

'Show me the shrink who doesn't. The mind is a very tricky fellow.'

'Indeed it is. Take Murphy's Law, for instance. If anything can go wrong, it will. But . . . does it make any sense? Suppose something is about to go wrong, Murphy's Law should step in and change the course of events, and make it right? You know what I mean? Look, Murphy's Law clearly states that if it can go wrong, it will – so, shouldn't that imply that something destined to go wrong, yes, it will go wrong, which is to say, it will not go wrong, it will correct itself, so to speak because Murphy says . . . tell me you do get my drift?'

'Sounds like some kind of a double negative, Mullah. Let's begin. Now, Mullah, you keep yourself busy with various projects, I believe? How is the mousetrap project coming along?'

'Not too good, I'm afraid. By the way, did you ever hear the expression, *If you give a mouse a cookie, he will always ask for a glass of milk.*'

'No. How would you describe your wife?'

'I don't deserve her.'

'How does she feel about this?'

'She agrees with me – one hundred per cent.'

'Does she agree with you on everything?' probed the psycho-analyst.

'No, this is the only matter on which we agree.'

'You don't have any children?'

'No. I blame England.'

'England?'

'It's a long story.'

The shrink began to take notes.

'I see. How would you describe your marriage?'

'Like a horse and carriage.'

'And which one of you is the horse?'

'I think that's enough for today, doc, don't you?'

'Before you go, Mullah: one last question, if I may.'

'You may.'

'What has life taught you, if anything?'

'Well, doc, I met an Irish priest once and I asked him the very same question. I was mightily impressed by his answer: experience is the comb, he said, that life gives a bald man.'

The shrink frowned. 'Thank you, Mullah. I'll try to figure that one out. If I can . . .'

The Mullah rose to leave.

'And the same priest, Fr. Campbell, knew a lot about that other question as well.'

'What other question?'

'Doc, a woman must want a man before she wants a baby. Isn't that so? If she lies back and thinks of England, that's no good, is it?'

'Why would she think of England? And whether she does, or not, has nothing to do with conception.'

'Ah, it's a long story.'

'Was the padre suggesting she should think of Ireland?'

'It's a long story.' The Mullah let himself out.

SOUP

'Ahmed!'

'What is it, Mullah? I'm very busy.'

'Yes, yes, everyone is busy. You think I'm not busy?'

'You, busy?'

'Never mind. Ahmed, why don't you have a soup named after me?'

'What? A soup named after you? Why should I have a soup named after you?'

'You have a soup named after another mullah. A nobody. A fake!'

'What soup? What mullah? What are you talking about?'

'It's there on your menu.'

'Where? Show it to me.'

'I haven't got my reading glasses with me. But CJ was raving about it. No. 11 on the menu.'

'Mullah, you idiot. That's Mulligatawny Soup!'

'Well, it's a disgrace! Who is he? I have asked around, Ahmed. Nobody has ever heard of this Gatawny fellow!'

BANNED

'I seem to be the only customer, Ahmed.'

'Yes, Mullah, you have my complete attention. What would you like?'

'Any jam?' asked the Mullah, hopefully.

'No jam, Mullah.'

'Tell me, Ahmed, did you always want to run a sandwich bar?'

'No, Mullah, when I was eighteen I wanted to form a group. A band.'

'Banned? Why am I not surprised?'

'No, Mullah, not banned. Band!'

'That's what I said. Now let's see, what am I going to have? I'll try the Mullah Gatawny soup. But don't tell anyone.'

POLITICS

'Actually,' said Nasrudin to the Chief Justice, 'I've got rather fond of this Mullah Gatawny soup. I'm quite addicted to it, I would say.'

'Delicious!' agreed the Chief Justice, slurping to his heart's content.

When he had finished the soup, the Chief Justice tapped the table nervously with his fingers.

'You seem a little on edge today, Your Honour?' remarked Nasrudin.

'Have you not seen the paper?' He handed Nasrudin the newspaper.

'Sorry, I haven't my reading glasses with me.'

'Another guerilla attack in the north east,' sighed CJ. 'Bloody awful.'

'Awful, I agree. I've always said they shouldn't let gorillas out of Africa. Keep them there, that's what I say.'

FORMS TO FILL IN

'We have some forms to fill in, I'm afraid,' said the shrink, 'that is if I am to go ahead and prescribe these new drugs for you.'

'Fine,' said Nasrudin. 'Fire ahead.'

'Wife's name?'

'It will come to me.'

'You don't know your – ?'

'Fatima! That's it . . . Or is that her sister, the one with the little dimple?'

'Nasrudin! This will not do at all. This is the 21st century.'

'21st century, eh? Well, I'm not very impressed so far, are you? Where were we? Wife's name . . . It's on the tip of my tongue, doc. Fatinah? Fathi? It must one of those. Put down Fat for short and we can't go wrong.'

The shrink clicked his tongue, disapprovingly.

'Fathi means 'open', as you know, doc, but open she ain't. No, sir! In fact, she's closed. Closed for business.'

'I put it to you, Nasrudin –'

'You put it to me, do you? We playing golf now?'

'I put it to you that you are a misogynist!'

'No! I am not a Ms. Ogynist, a Miss Ogynist or a Mrs Ogynist but I'll be a Mr Ogynist if you continue this line of questioning. Put that in your pipe and smoke it.'

The shrink sighed.

'Wife's profession?'

'None.'

'Your wife is a nun?'

PROGRESS

'Nasrudin,' said the shrink, 'I do believe we are making some progress but there's still a lot of work to be done, a few unresolved issues – your misogyny, for instance, and your Anglophobia. What is wrong with England? England, Nasrudin, England that gave us the Beatles?'

'The Beatles were Irish.'

'Oh, really? Well, what about Shakespeare?'

'Not according to J . T. Looney.'

'Who? Looney? You are making this up!'

'No no, doc. The father of your own science – psycho-analysis – Dr Freud; he, too, has questioned Shakespeare's authorship . . .'

'Freud who claimed that the Irish defy psycho-analysis?'

'That's a myth! Are you a Myth Ogynist, doc? A whole army of geniuses have questioned whether the bard ever wielded a quill in his life: Helen Keller, Charlie Chaplin, Fr Joey Campbell, Colonel Gaddafi, etc. My own belief is that all of Shakespeare, apart from the sonnets, was written by a gentleman by the name of O'Toole.'

'Come, come, Nasrudin. Looney, O'Toole . . . really!'

He paused.

'You are an unlikely Hibernophile, if I may say so.'

'My wife says the same thing. She has to go to her mother's on St. Patrick's Day.'

'Nasrudin . . . not your typical Irish name is it?'

'Oh,' said Nasrudin, haughtily, 'you'd be surprised. Nas- comes from the Irish, neas, meaning 'near'; rud- comes from the

Irish, rud, meaning 'a thing' or perhaps, *rúid* meaning 'a spurt'; and the final syllable, -in comes from the Irish *in* which is a diminutive suffix; so my name could mean 'near the little thing' or 'near the little spurt'.

The shrink took a deep breath.

'We have a lot of work to do, Nasrudin.'

'It never ends.'

WINSTON

The Chief of Police ran into Nasrudin at the bazaar.

'Ah, it's yourself,' said the wily policeman.

Nasrudin looked to the left and to the right, looked all around him, then looked up and down.

'Oh,' he said, 'are you talking to me?'

'I've had complaints about your donkey.'

'He has a name, you know.'

'A number of complaints, as a matter of fact. Let me see.'

He took out a little black book.

'Yes, here we are. Your neighbor, Siraj, who wishes to remain anonymous, claims that your donkey . . .'

'Winston, please!'

'He claims that your donkey smells. When did you last give him a wash?'

'Who? Winston or Siraj?'

'Don't be muddying the waters, Nasrudin!'

'Siraj wouldn't know his ass from his elbow. So, a Winstonian pong got up his nose? Yeah? What kind of a smell did he expect? Chanel No. 5? Really! Is it any wonder the whole world is laughing at us. Our beloved north-eastern province, famed in song and story, has been invaded by a band of left-wing gorillas and the police are concerned about donkey odour! Give me a break!'

INSURANCE

The Chief of Police knocked vigorously at the door. He was surrounded by several other policemen and one policewoman.

'Coming! Coming! Don't get your knickers in a knot!'

Nasrudin opened the door and, speaking to the policewoman, said. 'My apologies, my dear. I was not referring to you.' He turned to the Chief:

'What do *you* want?'

'Have you heard of insurance fraud, Nasrudin?'

'What are you on about?'

'You made an insurance claim a month ago regarding the unexpected death of your donkey.'

'Winston. Poor Winston . . . His likes will never be seen again.'

'Do I not see your Winston now, with my own two eyes? Is that not the aforementioned Winston, tethered to your fence?'

'Winston? No, no. That's his brother, Boris.'

'His brother?'

'Correct.'

'How do I know it's his brother?'

'How do you know it's not?'

THE CURIOUS CASE OF FR JOEY CAMPBELL

'What a world we live in,' exclaimed the Chief Justice. 'If it's not one thing, it's another.'

'And if it's not that, it's something else,' said Nasrudin who had been invited to CJ's bachelor pad for some refreshments and a natter.

'This spot of trouble in our smoldering north-eastern province is attracting a lot of unwanted attention, Nasrudin. Look at this rag from Hamburg. Stern magazine.' He threw the magazine angrily at Nasrudin.

'I can't read German,' apologized Nasrudin. Then he looked at the cover again.

'Some damned Irish priest, Nasrudin, has become the leader of those separatists up north. Can you believe it?'

'Good heavens!' exclaimed Nasrudin 'It's Fr. Campbell!'

'Yes, that's his name. How did you –?'

'Fr Joey Campbell. I'd know that little goatee anywhere!'

'You don't know this beast, surely!'

'Oh but I do! I do!'

It took a while for CJ to digest this extraordinary piece of information.

'Nasrudin! You actually know this fiend and his band of Joeyites? How?'

'We were in Mecca together, CJ.'

'What, on the hajj? He's a Muslim?'

'He's no more of a Muslim than Boris.'

'Who is Boris?'

'Boris is what I now call Winston. For insurance purposes.'

'It's hard to keep up with you, Nasrudin. Now listen, I need you to tell me everything you know about this Fr. Campbell monster. Our intelligence has nothing on him.'

'Of course, CJ. Fr Joey Campbell was born in a small farm in the west of Ireland and grew up as a normal boy, like any other boy really, except that he had 13 freckles on his nose, which was considered to be unlucky. His uncle, a Redemtorist priest, advised his mother to pray to St. Bartholomew, patron saint of Dermatology, and lo and behold, on his fourteenth birthday –'

'Cut to the chase, Nasrudin. We don't want to know what he has for his breakfast.'

'Mashed banana on brown bread – should you ever need to know. Anyway, Joey was exceptionally fond of the poc fada.'

'The what?'

'That's the long puck, CJ.'

'Not quite with you, Nasrudin.'

'Puck! In hurling, a game you play with a stick, the *poc fada* is competing with yourself, or others, to see how far you can puck the *sliotar*.'

'The what?'

'The ball.'

'Why didn't you say so?'

'But one day the *poc* fada hit a *poc*!'

'Again, Nasrudin, I'm afraid I don't quite follow you at all.'

'Did I say that poc means –'

'To hit the ball. Correct?'

'But it also means a goat.'

'Did you say a goat, Nasrudin?'

'Yes, a billy goat. Joey hit a goat. In the eye. With the *sliotar*. Gottit? The goat comes charging – and a Mayo billy goat is no joke – the goat comes charging and poor Joey, though agile enough it has to be said, poor Joey gets rammed.'

'What?'

'Rammed by the billy goat. A big horny fella.'

'Horned, perhaps?'

'That too. Terrible business. Joey was never quite the same again. He took it personally, you see. He saw it as an attack on his own person, by the devil himself. There's a wealth of songs, poems and ballads about the incident. My own favourite goes something like this:

> It was the morning of the fifteenth of September
> A day that we all will remember
> When Joey a boy with no fear
>> Approaching his fifteenth year
>> Didn't he let his sliotar fly
>> And hit a puck goat in the eye. ... '

'Let's leave the song until later, Nasrudin, shall we?'

'If you insist, CJ. So anyway, he undertook to devote his life to conquering the devil and overcoming evil. He joined the Holy Ghost order, and became an expert on O'Toole '

'O'Toole?'

'The man who wrote all of Shakespeare's plays.....'

CJ poured himself another stiff whiskey.

'It's all in one of his most hair-raising sermons, *Good and Evil: How I Was As Screwed Up As Hogan's Goat* '

'Sorry, who is Hogan?'

'I've no idea, CJ. I don't think Joey himself had the answer to that one. Anyway, get your friends in intelligence to study that sermon and you will know all you need to know about Joey.'

'This has been very helpful, Nasrudin. Very helpful indeed. We'll call on you if we need further information.'

'Let me know if your people find out more about Hogan's goat, CJ. It keeps me up at night '

'You'll be the first to know, Nasrudin.'

CJ rubbed his chin, thoughtfully.

'I've heard that this padre of yours is a bit of a maverick, Nasrudin. Would you agree?'

'You know what Mohyuddin Ibn 'Arabi says?'

'Ah, you have studied the greatest Sheikh of them all, the Shaykh ul Aakbar?'

'Naturally, CJ, I am a Mullah after all. When I think of Fr Joey, I think of something said by the Sheik:

In the east, he saw the lightning and yearned for the east, but if it had flashed in the west he would have yearned for the west . . . '

'Beautiful, Nasrudin. But what does it mean?'

'I haven't the foggiest notion, CJ!'

NEGOTIATIONS

'Lunch is on me today,' said CJ.

'I'm very much obliged to Your Honour.'

'Think nothing of it, Nasrudin.'

'Nothing it is then, CJ.'

The Chief Justice looked around cautiously.

'Nasrudin,' he whispered, conspiratorially, 'I've been talking to some people in very high places.'

'How high, CJ? This high?' Nasrudin put his hand a few inches above his head.

CJ indicated with his index finger that he should go higher.

'This high?'

CJ indicated higher and higher until Nasrudin's hand couldn't go any higher.

Ahmed came to the table.

'There is something you require, gentlemen?'

'A little privacy, if possible,' said CJ with an air of importance.

'Certainly!' said Ahmed, retreating.

'Nasrudin, I don't believe in tergiversation.'

'Who does?' asked Nasrudin who had never heard the word before.

'So, I'll get straight to the point. We want you to negotiate with Fr Joey.'

'Me? Negotiate?'

Nasrudin was bewildered.

'Why me?'

'You know him. You were on the pilgrimage together. How did he manage that, by the way?'

'Oh, you'd be surprised the places he can get into. He told me he once managed to get into the Vatican.'

'I see . . . Look, Nasrudin, we want this fighting to stop. They can have their stupid little province. It's not that's its bursting at the seams with oil or anything like that! It's nothing but mountains and hills. We just want the fighting to stop. We have our reasons which we needn't go into now. The fighting must stop. Do you understand? We are under pressure.'

'USA?' asked Nasrudin, raising an eybrow.

'China.   So, you just tell those North Easties they can have their independence, their own language, whatever they want. Why would they want their own language when they can have ours – for free.'

'Nothing is free, CJ.'

'Do you know what they call a car in their language? *Kar!* Can you believe it?'

'From the Irish, carbad, meaning a chariot.'

'Really? Anyway, Nasrudin, we want you to go there, talk to Fr Joey and his guerillas and ask them to lay down their arms.'

'Gorillas have very big arms, don't they?'

'Yes, Nasrudin. They do.'

'What's in it for me?'

'We thought ......50 donkeys?'

'Wow ...... that's a lot of donkeys. A lot of responsibility. How about 40?'

'40 it is then, Nasrudin. If you are imprisoned, tortured or beheaded, the government will disavow your actions. You will be on your own.'

'I very much look forward to meeting Fr Joey again. I see him as my mentor in many ways. It was he who explained my title to me, Mullah.'

'Oh, really?'

'From the Irish, *mullach*, meaning 'top'. Top dog, CJ, head honcho!'

'I never doubted it for a moment!'

'He gave me this button. It's from a French soldier's uniform. I carry it everywhere I go.'

'What is its significance?' asked CJ, examining the relic.

'It's from the time of the Republic of Connaught.'

'Never heard of it.'

'It only lasted 12 days. But Fr Joey's ancestors were in the thick of it. A brilliant Franco-Hiberno assault on British forces in Mayo.'

~

When he got home, Nasrudin was more excited than he had ever been in all his married life:

'Wife, as you know, I don't believe in tergiversation.'

'You don't believe in anything, Nasrudin.'

'So, I'll get straight to the point. I have been asked by the government to talk to Fr. Joey. They will give me 40 donkeys for my trouble.'

'They are offloading donkeys on you now? This is the 21st century, husband. The day of the donkey is well and truly over. What were you going to do with 40 donkeys? The donkey-for-hire business is finished, Nasrudin. It has been over for years. When did someone last ask for the loan of Winston for the day?'

'Boris.'

'Boris?'

'He is Boris now since the in – '

'The *in* what? What are you trying to say?'

'Since the . . . ins . . .'

'*Ins* . . .?'

'Insubordination.'

'Whatever. We don't want 40 donkeys, Nasrudin. And we

don't want buttons either. Renegotiate.'
    'What do we want?'
    'Money!'
    'Money can't buy me love, my dear.'
    'Neither can donkeys!'

SILVER

Two months after Nasrudin's successful negotiations with Fr Joey and his freedom fighters, CJ and Nasrudin were happily slurping soup in Ahmed's famous Fancy Sandwich Bar when a courier arrived with a package for CJ.

CJ looked at the padded envelope with an air of foreboding.

'Excuse me one moment,' he said as he began to open the envelope, nervously. It was a copy of *Stern*. CJ looked at the cover. His eyes became glazed:

'Why are we always the last to know?' he said, despairingly.

Thecoverstoryhadaphotoofajoyous Fr Joeyandthelegend underneath declared that the tiny province – now enjoying political independence after a short-lived revolutionary struggle – had discovered what scientists believe may be the largest quantity of silver in modern mining history.

CHICKEN

'Ah,' said CJ. 'Chicken noodle soup.'

They were both hungry. It was a pleasure to see them devour their soup with such zest. When they finished, Nasrudin said, 'Tell me, CJ, why did the chicken cross the road?'

'I don't know, Nasrudin!'

'Well, certainly not to get to Ahmed's place!'

They laughed heartily, both of them glancing at Ahmed, who scowled because he thought they were laughing at him.

'Fr Joey once said that the chicken never crossed the road in the first place.'

'I am not a great fan of Fr Joey, as you know.'

'Fr Joey says he has proof that the chicken never crossed the road. He was pushed!'

ANTHOLOGY

'Another coffee, Nasrudin?'

'I don't mind if I do, CJ.'

'I have been asked by a prominent publisher to put together an anthology of political quotations.'

'How exciting!' enthused Nasrudin.

'I thought I'd read you a little selection of some of my favourites, said the Chief Justice.'

'Bring them on, CJ.'

'Let's start with Plato.'

'The potato? Fr Joey says there never was a famine in Ireland. Did you know that? The potato failed, yes, but that was only one crop. 67 regiments of the British Army oversaw the export of all kinds of foodstuffs to . . .'

'Let me interrupt you there, Nasrudin. Plato, I said. Not potato.'

'Ah, Plato! Of course. Plato, one of my favourites.'

'Plato says: "One of the penalties for refusing to participate in politics is that you end up being governed by your inferiors." What do you think?'

'And if you *do* participate in politics, CJ, does that mean you end up being governed by your superiors?'

'I see what you mean, Nasrudin . . . That could be problematic.'

'Not for our superiors.'

'We'll park Plato for the moment. Let's move along, shall we? "Perseverance is the hard work you do after you get tired of doing the hard work you already did." What do you think of that one, Nasrudin?'

'I don't like it, CJ. There's something wrong with it.'

'What do you mean?'

'It's a bit off.'

'In what way?'

'Who said it?'

'Newt Gingrich.'

'Ah, there, you see! That's what's wrong with it.

Newt is not a name, CJ! A newt is a type of small salamander with unreliable legs that lives on alcohol.'

'Really?'

'Have you never heard the expression, as pissed as a newt?'

'Moving on . . . I really am glad I consulted you on this, Nasrudin. The whole thing could have turned into a disaster. Sometimes you don't see what's right there in front of your eyes.'

'Tell me about it.'

'OK, that's Plato and Gingrich gone. Now, let's see: "If voting changed anything, they'd make it illegal." Emma Goldman. Oh no, what was I thinking? No, no, we can't have that sort of thing. Out, damned spot! That's three gone already, I'm afraid. Nasrudin . . .?'

'CJ . . .?'

'What is happening to our anthology?'

'Your anthology, CJ . . . Have the publishers paid you an advance?'

'I'm not free to discuss it, Nasrudin.'

'More than 40 donkeys, probably?'

'Here's one: "The modern conservative is engaged in one of man's oldest exercises in moral philosophy, that is, the search for a superior moral justification for selfishness." John Kenneth Galbraith. Oh no! What prompted me to use that quotation? This is worse than intolerable.'

'I don't like people who use a middle name, CJ. John Galbraith wasn't enough for him. He had to ruin it all with Kenneth. People never know when they have enough, CJ. That's why I hate Picasso. Do you know what his full name was? Pablo Diego José Francisco de Paula Juan Nepomuceno María de los Remedios Cipriano de la Santísima Trinidad Ruiz y Picasso. What a *tonto*.'

'You can say that again!'

'Pablo Diego José Francisco de Paula Juan Nepomuceno María de los Remedios Cipriano de la Santísima Trinidad Ruiz y Picasso.'

CJ looked at the John Kenneth Galbraith quote and, sadly, put a line through it. A fourth quotation had quietly bitten the dust.

He began to perspire. Nasrudin handed him an FSB serviette with which he quickly mopped his brow.

'How about this one: "Politics is the art of looking for trouble, finding it everywhere, diagnosing it incorrectly and applying all the wrong remedies." Ernest Benn. Nope! Gone!'

'Well, at least, CJ, it wasn't Ernest de la Santísima Trindad Ruiz Tonto y Benn, or something like that!'

'Goodbye, Mr Benn, whoever you are. . . That's five in a row.'

'Five in a row? Oh, that's a good one, CJ. I like the sound of that.'

'Is there any point in going on?'

'Another good one. Who said that?'

'No, Nasrudin. That was me asking whether . . . Never mind. Back to the drawing bord, I guess.'

'Back to the drawing board? Another keeper, CJ. You're on a roll!'

ANTHOLOGY [II]

The following day, CJ and Nasrudin continued their analysis of the ever-shrinking anthology of political quotes over a long lunch.

'My name will be on it, Nasrudin. I must be very careful. I'm the Chief Justice, after all. A public intellectual. There's a lot riding on this. Here we go, then: "Since a politician never believes what he says, he is quite surprised to be taken by his word." Charles de Gaulle.'

'He had a lot of gall, didn't he?' opined Nasrudin.

'Sadly, he too will have to go.' And CJ drew a red line through the quotation. 'I'm getting worried, Nasrudin. I may not have the makings of an anthology at all at this rate. What's this one? G. K. Chesterton: "Tradition means giving votes to the most obscure of all classes, our ancestors." What do you think, Nasrudin?'

'It's deep, CJ. No harm in it if readers don't get it, is there? People don't actually think today, do they? As long as they buy the book. That's what counts.'

'True. Many a mickle makes a muckle.'

'You've taken the words out of my mouth.'

'The publishers say we must have a gender spread and a geographical spread in the anthology, Nasrudin. Now, here's Mikhail Gorbachev: "I paid too heavy a price for perestroika."'

'Perestroika?' asks Nasrudin, quizzically. 'Some kind of vodka, is it?'

'Moving on . . . Patrice Lumumba: "We know that Africa is neither French, nor British, nor American, nor Russian, that it is African . . ."

'I like it, CJ.'

'Good. We're sucking diesel.'

'That's a good one too, CJ. Leave that one in . . . I'm worried about something, though. Run some of those names by me again . . .'

'Sure. Patrice Lumumba . . . Mikhail Gorbachev . . . Charles de Gaulle . . .'

'Suppose, CJ, suppose they never said any of those things.'

'What do you mean?'

'I mean, suppose they had a team of speechwriters, working for them day and night. Boss! Boss! How about this one, boss: "Africa is neither French, nor British nor . . ." See what I mean? Some poor speechwriter, working all his life and then they hand him a pension of 20 donkeys. He's the real hero here, if you ask me. Not Charles Lumumba or Patrice de Gaulle or that other fella . . .'

'Good point, Nasrudin, but I'm afraid I can't deal with it now. So, moving on . . . Aristophanes, Nasrudin?'

'I beg your pardon?'

'Shall we try Aristophanes?'

'No thanks, I'll just have another croissant, CJ, if I may.'

'Aristophanes: "Under every stone lurks a politician." '

'CJ? Did you put this anthology together yourself?'

'Of course not, Nasrudin. Don't be silly. Why do you think I have a secretary? Most of this stuff I'm seeing here for the first time. Oh! How did *he* get in here?'

'Who?'

'Your friend, Fr Joey Campbell.'

'He's in it?'

'Not for long!'

'What does he say?'

Oh . . . it's not really a quote. It's a quote within a quote.

What's called a gluote.'

'A gluote?'

'Yes, your friend invented it. It's when you use a quote to gloat about something.'

'Let's hear it, please!'

'It appears that he uses the opening lines of a poem by one Walter de la Mare, *Silver*, to gloat over the newly-found riches of his adopted country:

> "Slowly, silently, now the moon
> Walks the night in her silver shoon;
> This way, and that, she peers and sees
> Silver fruit upon silver trees . . ." '

'I'm beginning to feel rather ill, Nasrudin.'

'*Silver*! He quotes it all the time, CJ. One of their poets – she has long silvery hair, as it happens – she's translated it into their own language and now it's their national anthem. They love it in the north east of the North Eastern province, but the north west and the south all have different dialects, so it hasn't gone down at all well in other parts, unfortunately:

> "One by one the casements catch
> Her beams beneath the silvery thatch;
> Couched in his kennel, like a log,
> With paws of silver sleeps the dog;
> From their shadowy cote the white breasts peep
> Of doves in a silver-feathered sleep;
> A harvest mouse goes scampering by,
> With silver claws, and silver eye;
> A moveless fish in the water gleams
> By silver reeds in a silver stream . . ." '

'Nasrudin, stop; you *must* stop. I'm feeling rather faint.'

PAWNSHOP

'You what?' said Nasrudin? 'You pawned the radio?'

'What was I to do?' protested Fatima. 'Conjure up a meal – like a rabbit out of a top hat? Get me a top hat! I am desperate enough to try anything!'

'What do we want with top hats? Are we British toffs? Hmm . . . Rabbit did you say? I haven't eaten rabbit in years . . .'

'Well, go catch one!'

'With my bad hip? I am to become a rabbit-catcher?' Nasrudin waited outside the pawnshop until a minute before mid-day before making his grand entrance.

'Hello, Mullah,' said the pawnbroker respectfully.

'Just checking on our radio. Still working?'

'No collateral damage, if that's what you mean, Mullah.'

The pawnbroker switched on the radio. Loud heavy-metal music was playing. The Mullah frowned.

The pawnbroker apologised immediately and began fiddling with the dial.

'That's it!' said Nasrudin. 'The twelve o'clock news.'

He listened to the news from start to finish and thanked the pawnbroker before making a breezy exit:

'I'll be back again same time tomorrow!'

JAM

'Ahmed?'

'Yes, Nasrudin, what is it?' replied the owner of FSB (Famous Sandwich Bar. Or was it Fancy Sandwich Bar? The owner himself, Ahmed, had forgotten. Only the sign remained, FSB).

'What does FSB stand for?'

'Fabled Sandwich Bar? You have asked me this so many times, Nasrudin, that I myself am getting confused. Fantastic? Fascinating? Fathomless? Any suggestions?'

'How about Favourite, Ahmed?'

'That's a good one. Fortunate?'

'Friendly?'

'Yes, Nasrudin, that's it. Friendly!'

'Well, you should live up to your name. Be friendly. Have complimentary jam containers for your customers.'

'So you can bring them home to your wife?'

'Listen Ahmed, wherever he went, Edward Said would bring home little jam containers and spread jam on his homemade English muffins. Though, what's so great about English muffins, I cannot say.'

'What did Edward Said himself say about them?'

'Said? Said nothing.'

FIRST DATE

'Nasrudin, your son is having his first date this evening.'

'I have a son?'

'Nasrudin! He is 14 years of age and this evening he's having his first date. So please be serious and act as a father for a change.'

'Son, where are you? Come here!'

A gawky youth appeared.

'You? Oh yes, you. Sure, I've seen you around. I thought . . . never mind. So, first date this evening, yeah?'

'Yes, daddy.'

He called me daddy, said Nasrudin to himself, and his chest began to expand with pride.

'I have a little present for you, my son.'

He disappeared and returned after five minutes, with something wrapped in fancy coloured paper.

'I hope your first date goes well, my son. Whether it does or not, I know you will never forget your second date. Here you are my son, a Medjool date, the best there is – I've been keeping it especially for you!'

NEWS

'Good afternoon, CJ!'

'Ah' exclaimed the Chief Justice, grinning broadly, 'it's the Mullah Nasrudin.'

CJ lay his newspaper aside.

'I don't know why you waste money on that!'

said Nasrudin, contemptuously.

'The Times?'

'Have you never heard the old proverb? *Do not buy either the moon or the news, for in the end they will both come out.*'

'No, Nasrudin. That's a new one on me. But I see from *The Times* that your old friend Fr Joey has made himself President for Life.'

He picked up the newspaper again, opened page 3, and showed Nasrudin a photograph of his friend and hero.

'I don't like his smile, Nasrudin. He has a wry little mouth.'

'That's the meaning of Campbell, CJ, in both Irish and Scots Gaelic: *cam* is crooked and *béal* is mouth. All the Campbells have crooked mouths. And all the Camerons have crooked noses.'

'What? Every Campbell has a crooked mouth and every Cameron a crooked nose? Is that what you're saying?

'Do you want a straight answer, CJ?

THE END OF LOVE

It was their wedding anniversary but, unfortunately, it had slipped Nasrudin's mind.

'Nasrudin, is this what I had in mind on my wedding day? That it would end like this?'

'Fatima, what are you saying?! Never think of beginning or end. What did Farid ud-Din Attar say?'

'What?'

'Fool,' he said, 'there's no destination! Loved one and lover and love are eternal.'

A voice was heard:
'Nothing but Sufistry and sophistry'
'Son,' said Nasrudin, 'you shouldn't be eavesdropping!'

WHAT'S IN A NAME?

The shrink was chewing his pencil.

'Nasrudin,' he said finally, 'do you show any affection for your wife? Do you kiss her?'

'Doc, if I were kissing her, my name wouldn't be Nasrudin. It would be Kissinger.'

EARTH TO NASRUDIN

'Can I get you another coffee, Nasrudin?' asked Ahmed.
No reply.
'Nasrudin? Hello?'
No reply.
Ahmed shook him by the shoulder.
'Earth to Nasrudin. Come in Nasrudin.'
'Ah, Ahmed . . .'
'You'll have another coffee? I thought you were in some kind of a swoon there for a while, my friend. I was saying to myself, Is he here at all?"
'You know what Shah Niaz says?'
'No, I'm afraid not.'

> '*Everything is illusion, a mirage:*
> *I know I do not exist . . . yet doubt persists.*'

'Is that a yes or a no, Nasrudin?'
'Yes, I suppose I might as well have another coffee . . . while I'm here.

STRAY DOG

Nasrudin brought home a stray dog. His son was delighted:

'For me, daddy?'

'Yes my son. You may call the dog Amir.'

'Why Amir, daddy?'

'To remind you of what Amir Khusrow Dehlavi says:

Friendship with a dog - less pain
Than friendship with men who are arrogant and vain!'

'True, husband,' said Fatima, examining the flea-bitten cur, 'but let's not forget the words of Mahmud Shabistari:

Knowledge of faith springs from angelic virtues,
It enters not a heart with a dog's nature.'

The boy spoke up:

'Do I get to keep the bloody dog or not?'

'Of course you get to keep the bloody dog!' insisted Nasrudin. 'But in deference to your mother, call him Amir today, and tomorrow Mahmud; Amir again the following day and so on . . .'

'Why don't I just call him Joey,' said the boy. He went to the door, turned back, and whistled to the dog:

'Come on, Joey!'

'What time is it?' asked Nasrudin, suddenly.

'Almost noon,' said Fatima.

'Don't let that dog out!' warned Nasrudin. 'He might go mad!'

'What do you mean, father?' asked the boy.

'Ah, my son, you have a lot to learn: mad dogs and Englishmen go out in the midday sun!'

PHANTOM TURBAN

'Fatima, beloved, an emergency! Birds have gone and soiled my turban once again. Could you possibly give it a good cleaning and ironing? I wouldn't think of bringing it to the dry cleaners. It's unbelievable what they charge.'

'You are perfectly capable of cleaning your own turban, beloved! I have an important meeting with the Society for 21st Century Women.'

Never heard of them, remarked Nasrudin to himself.

Later that day, Ahmed remarked that Nasrudin was looking a little pale.

'Are you OK, Mullah?'

'What is OK, Ahmed? Are you OK? Is anybody OK? What does OK even mean?'

'OK means OK, Mullah.'

'Pete Seeger says it's a Choctaw word but Fr Joey insists it's an Ulster Scots expression: Och aye! Anyway, have you ever heard of a phantom limb?'

'You mean – ?

'Yes, Ahmed, as when a leg is missing and you can still feel a sensation or pain where the limb once was.'

'Mullah, I did not notice that you were missing a leg. What happened?'

'Nothing. I have two legs under me, Ahmed, don't worry.'

'And Winston is OK?'

'Boris. He's fine. No, it's my head.'

'Your head?'

'I had to remove my turban. To wash it. The syndrome is known as 'phantom turban'. The head, not accustomed to being without a turban, begins to act very strangely.'

'Phantom turban, Mullah? Is there any cure for it?'

'Och aye! The turban must be returned to the head as soon as possible.'

SURVEY

A knock came to the door.

'Hello,' said a cheerful but gawkish young man, 'we're doing a survey in the area. Would you care to participate? It won't take a minute.'

'Shoot!' said Nasrudin.

'I wish someone would!' said Fatima. Nasrudin stepped outside and closed the door.

'Who was that?' asked the surveyor.

'Oh, that was my parrot. She's a member of the Society for 21st Century Parrots. Don't take a bit of notice of her.'

'OK, now, let's see. You may answer 'Yes' or 'No', 'Rather Not Say', 'Unsure,' or 'None of the Above'.

'Name?'

'Mullah Nasrudin. Mullah means 'top dog' but everyone says my bark is worse than my bite.'

'Address?'

'Rather not say.'

'Age?'

'Unsure.'

'Marital status?'

'Och, aye.'

'What was that?'

'Unsure.'

'Profession?'

'Mullah.'

'Do you keep any pets?'

'No.'

'You neighbour mentioned a donkey. Winston, is it?'

'No, Siraj.'

'What?'

'My neighbour's name is Siraj.'

'The donkey!'

'No, the donkey's name is Boris. Not exactly a pet.'

'What about the parrot?'

'What parrot?'

'Didn't you just mention a parrot a while ago?'

'Rather not say.'

'Hobbies?'

'Haiku.'

'A form of self-defense, is it?'

'Here's one I submitted to *Modern Haiku* but it wasn't modern enough for them:

> morning rain . . .
> the donkey's coat
> changes colour

'Politically speaking, would you say you lean to the left, or to the right? Or would you be centre?'

'None of the above.'

'Your neighbour says you are a Joeyite. Would that be correct?'

'My neighbour! Ask Siraj about his cockroaches.'

'He has cockroaches?'

'Rather not say.'

CHANGE OF MENU

'You know, Ahmed, I've been thinking . . .'

'Hmm . . .?'

'Top dogs need a change of menu now and again. You can't have the same menu year in year out.'

'What top dogs, Mullah?'

'CJ and . . . myself . . . and . . . as you know, the Irish ambassador is going to turn up on St. Patrick's Day.'

'I'll believe it when I see it. What change were you thinking about?'

'Everyone is talking about health foods these days, Ahmed. Shitake mushrooms, for instance.'

'I'll look into it. How do you spell these mushrooms?'

'M-U-S-H –'

'No, the other word.'

'Oh yes, of course. You are writing this down?'

'Yes, go ahead, Mullah.'

'S-H-I – '

'S-HI –'

'T-A-K-E.'

　'T-A-K-E.'

　'Read it back to me.'

'S-H-I-T –'

'No! That is not what I said, Ahmed. Start again!

　'S-H-I –'

'S-H-I –'

'T-A-K-E.'

　'T-A-K-E'

'That's it. Now read it back, please.
    'S-H-I-T –'
'Ahmed! You are impossible!'

A DIPLOMATIC INCIDENT

The Mullah had invited the Irish ambassador, Jeremiah O'Toole, Esq. to an official lunch in FSB for St. Patrick's Day. His Excellency graciously accepted.

'You will join us?' he asked CJ, eagerly.

'I wouldn't miss it for anything,' promised the Chief Justice. 'Though that Ambassador O'Toole fellow is not the jolliest Irishman I've ever met.'

'I agree. Educated in Oxford. He's hardly an Irishman at all, but as we're having a little shindig on St. Patrick's Day, we cannot but invite him.'

'A shindig?'

'Without the dancing.'

'If there's even the smell of alcohol, Nasrudin, I'll have to close the place down. You realize that?'

'Of course, CJ. It will all be kosher, if you pardon the expression. I've left it all to Ahmed. He's quite excited about it, really. The first ever St. Patrick's Day lunch in FSB. He is preparing a few surprises, he says.'

The great day arrived. Ahmed had rolled out a green carpet at the entrance. CJ, the Mullah and Ahmed himself greeted the Ambassador on his arrival, a man with a tendency to act above his station.

'Your Excellency,' Ahmed bowed extravagantly, 'welcome to our first ever St. Patrick's Day shindig.'

The Ambassador took no notice of him and was about to accept CJ's extended hand when he spotted something – a photograph taken out of a magazine and framed above the cash register, with the words, FAMOUS IRISH WRITER.

'Who is that?' said Ambassador O'Toole, brusquely.

'Joyce, your Excellence.'

'Not Joyce,' said O'Toole.

'Not Joyce?' said Ahmed.

'Not Joyce,' repeated O'Toole.

'Yes, Joyce,' insisted Ahmed.

'Take it down immediately. That is not James Joyce. It's William Joyce, aka Lord Haw Haw, Irish-American Nazi propagandist.'

CJ and the Mullah exchanged nervous glances.

'Not famous writer?' asked Ahmed, shattered.

Ambassador O'Toole glared at him.

Ahmed took down the photo and unceremoniously dumped it in the rubbish bin.

'And stay there!' thundered Ahmed. He then began to crow: 'Haw haw! Who is having the last haw-haw now, eh?' And, turning to his illustrious guests, he said 'My deepest apologies, please let me show you to your table.'

Before the ambassador sat down, he groaned and said, 'And what is this pathetic-looking vegetable, pray?' pointing at a leek in a vase.

'Too short notice to get shamrock,' said Ahmed. 'Got leek instead. It's good?'

'The leek,' said the Ambassador, sneeringly, 'is a Welsh symbol. Please get rid of it.'

'Certainly, Your Excellence,' said a humbled Ahmed.

'Your Excellency!' the Ambassador corrected him.

'Your Excellency? Thank you, Your Excellence.'

Ahmed withdrew and, with a vengeance, smashed the leek on top of the photo of Lord Haw Haw.

Itwasn'tgoingwell. CJtriedtomakesomelightconversation.

Ambassador O'Toole ignored him. It was now the Mullah's turn:

'Fr Joey is doing quite well for himself, isn't he, Your Excellence . . . I mean, Your Excellency?'

Ambassador O'Toole rose and said, 'Will you excuse me, gentlemen?' and walked out. He was whisked away in a Mercedes.

Ahmed arrived with a large plate of green Yorkshire pudding.

'Where is his Excellence?'

'He had another engagement.'

Ahmed's face fell.

'A pity. Anyway, my friends, enjoy your meal,' he said, deflated.

'What is this?' asked CJ, prodding the pudding with a fork.

'Yorkshire pudding. Yorkshire is in Ireland, no?'

The other two shook their heads dolefully.

Ahmed had tears in his eyes.

'I even learned an Irish song for the occasion . . . and now his Excellence is not even here to hear it.'

CJ humoured him:

'Forget his Excellence. We're here, Ahmed. You will sing it for us, won't you?'

Ahmed began to sing. What a pathetic sight he was, poor man, the tears almost choking him. He only managed the first six lines before becoming hopelessly confused:

> My father and mother were Irish
> And I am Irish too
> I bought a wee fiddle for ninepence
> And it is Irish too:
> I'm up in the morning early
> To meet the dawn of day . . .
> And the Mullah has 'phantom turban'
> But he says it'll go away . . .